My Prairie Summer

Acknowledgments

Executive Editor	Stephanie Muller
Product Manager	Wendy Whitnah
Senior Supervising Editor	Carolyn Hall
Senior Design Manager	Pamela Heaney
Contributing Editor	Donna Rodgers
Electronic Production Artist	Bo McKinney
Program Author	Gare Thompson

Library of Congress Cataloging-in-Publication Data
Glasscock, Sarah, 1952–
  My prairie summer / written by Sarah Glasscock; illustrated by Ed Martinez.
    p.   cm.
  Summary: A young prairie farm girl records her summer adventures in a diary.
  ISBN 0-8172-5161-8
  [1. Diaries — Fiction.   2. Bison — Fiction.   3. Prairies — Fiction.
  4. Farm life — Fiction.]   I. Martinez, Ed, ill.   II. Title.
  PZ7.G48135My   1998
  [E] — dc21
                                                97-23066
                                                CIP   AC

1 2 3 4 5 6 7 8 9 F 01 00 99 98 97

My Prairie Summer

Written by Sarah Glasscock
Illustrated by Ed Martinez

RSVP ®

RAINTREE
STECK-VAUGHN
PUBLISHERS
The Steck-Vaughn Company

Austin, Texas

Contents

Going to Get Lucy

June 6, Morning

Dear Diary,
*   We are on the way to pick up Lucy today! Mom, Dad, Ty, and I left the farm this morning. I sat in the back seat and watched the trailer wag behind our truck.*
*   On the way, Ty spotted a jackrabbit. Dad saw a hawk. Mom saw some purple coneflowers and pulled off the road. Everybody got out but me. I'm still sitting in the truck writing. Mom must be taking a million pictures! I sure wish they would hurry up. Lucy is waiting!*

FINALLY! I thought they'd never get back in the truck. Now we're going again. We just drove through a town. Mom always acts like she knows everybody. She was even waving at strangers. I ducked my head so they wouldn't see me.

Ty made me so mad when we drove past the town pool. Mom asked me if I was going to take swimming lessons this summer. Before I could even answer, Ty yelled that I wasn't because I was AFRAID! I'm not afraid. Well, maybe I'm a little scared of water.

5

June 6, Afternoon

Dear Diary,
    Well, we made it to Leon Biggelo's ranch. I was so excited that I jumped right out of the truck and ran up to the porch. Leon came out laughing because I was in such a hurry. He took us out back to see Lucy. She is so beautiful! She is as tall as me and has brown hair and brown eyes. But she already weighs four hundred pounds! Lucy is our new buffalo! We will protect her on our ranch. She can run free on the plains.
    I laughed when I saw Leon's sign:
BIGGELO BUFFALO RANCH!

I asked Leon when Lucy was born. He said her birthday was in May. Me, too! Now we can celebrate our birthdays together. Leon showed me how to hold out long stems of grass so Lucy could eat them. She wrapped her tongue around them and ate them all! I wanted to get going so Lucy could meet our other buffaloes. But we had to stay and talk with Leon awhile. Dad and Leon led Lucy into the trailer. She was finally mine! Well, I mean OURS.

Ty and Mom went swimming at the pond when we got home. Not me. I stayed with Dad and helped feed Lucy. I hope she likes it here.

The Big Storm

July 11, Morning

Dear Diary,
    Something was wrong with Lucy this morning. I held out a blade of bluestem grass, but she wouldn't eat it. Dad said Lucy was fine. He said that Lucy was just too hot to eat. Boy, it IS hot today!
    Dad said going swimming would cool me off. I know what that means. It's time for my swimming lesson. I'd rather pick grasshoppers off the corn plants than swim. I am a little scared of the water, but I don't want Ty to know. Ty swims like a fish. He sort of looks like one, too. HA, HA!

11

July 11, Afternoon

Dear Diary,

    I ALMOST floated today! Well, when Dad let go of me, I started to sink. I think I drank the whole pond. I came up coughing. Dad said maybe that was enough for one day. We got out of the water. Ty made his usual "quack, quack" noise, but none of the ducks quacked back. Now that was strange! The ducks always quacked with Ty. But today they seemed afraid of something.

    Suddenly it got dark, so I looked up. A huge, black cloud was moving across the sky. It was a like a giant mountain, all tall and wide.

Dad told us to throw on our clothes and get going fast. I could tell he thought this would be a bad storm. We ran home. Just before we got home, the clouds got darker and darker. The wind blew dust in our faces. It started raining on us. We raced to the storm cellar. Mom was already there. She grabbed us all up in a tight hug and kissed us. I was scared. Ty was scared now, too.

The rain and hail pounded against the storm cellar door. I didn't think it would ever stop. Mom sang songs with us, but I think she was scared, too. Dad kept checking the latch on the door. Finally, it was quiet outside. Dad slowly opened the door. Everything seemed to be okay. Some shutters had come off our house. The animals in the barn were a little scared, but they were all right. Best of all, Lucy was okay!

Lucy Runs Away

August 2

Dear Diary,

   Lucy ran away today! Ty opened the gate and she pushed right past him. It wasn't Ty's fault, but he was upset. I was out riding my horse, Daisy, so I went after Lucy. Ty, Mom, and Dad jumped in the truck and went after her, too. Lucy ran into the cornfield. The corn is taller than Dad now, so we couldn't see Lucy. Dad thought that maybe she would stop to eat because the corn is so sweet now. We all hoped she would.

I was scared for Lucy. Dad, Mom, and Ty drove around to one side of the field. I rode around to the other side. Lucy heard us and ran out of the field. Everyone else chased after her. I jumped off Daisy and stayed in the field in case Lucy turned around and came back. The tall grass brushed against me. The tiny bobwhites flew out of the grass. Lucy was heading for the pond. Now I was really scared. Lucy didn't know how to swim. Then I heard a loud splash!

I found Daisy and rode to the pond as
fast as I could. I was sure something bad
had happened to Lucy. By the time I got
there, everybody was in the water. I slid
off Daisy and ran to the pond. Lucy was
swimming! I couldn't believe it. There she
was swimming with Mom, Dad, and Ty. I
just jumped in and started swimming with
all of them.

Now both Lucy and I can swim!
Great, huh? I'm sure glad Lucy is okay.

August 15

Dear Diary,

Today is really dry and dusty. It's a good thing I learned to swim this summer. That's the best way to cool off on a hot prairie day. Lucy even went to the pond with Ty and me this afternoon. Ty showed me how to swim underwater. Maybe he isn't such a bad brother after all.

School starts next week, so I'll only see Lucy after school. Maybe we'll have some adventures together this fall. When we do, I'll be sure to write it all down here.

Emma